SPIRIT SURPRISE

LINDA CHAPMAN
Illustrated by Hoang Giang

LITTLE TIGER
LONDON

MAGIC KEEPERS

SPIRIT SURPRISE

To the lovely Philippa Milnes-Smith from The Soho Agency who loved and encouraged this series from the start. I feel so lucky to have had you as my agent and friend! – L. C.

To Ren, for always being by my side. – H. G.

LITTLE TIGER
An imprint of Little Tiger Press Limited
1 Coda Studios, 189 Munster Road, London SW6 6AW

Imported into the EEA by Penguin Random House Ireland,
Morrison Chambers, 32 Nassau Street, Dublin D02 YH68

A paperback original
First published in Great Britain in 2023

ISBN: 978-1-78895-477-8

A CIP catalogue record for this book is available from the British Library.

Printed and bound in the UK.

10 9 8 7 6 5 4 3 2 1

CONTENTS

CHAPTER ONE

"Magic is real," said Sarah, shaking her head. "Magic is actually real. I still can't believe it."

Ava and Lily grinned at each other. They had heard Sarah say the same thing at least a hundred times over the last two days – ever since she'd helped them capture an ancient crocodile mummy that had come to life.

Excitement fizzed through Ava. Her life had changed so much since she and her mum had moved into Curio House. The rambling old Victorian villa had once belonged to Enid

Pennington, an archaeologist, but on her death she had left the house and her collection of strange curios to Ava's mum, her great-niece. Ava and her mum had moved in three weeks ago only for Ava to discover something amazing – the curios were magic!

"But how can the rest of the world not know magic exists?" Sarah went on, shifting her school bag on her shoulder as the three of them walked to Ava's house after school on Friday.

Ava shrugged. "I don't know. Maybe because the people who know about it try to keep it secret, like Great-Aunt Enid did."

Lily gave an excited skip, making her dark hair bounce on her shoulders. "We're going to keep it secret too, aren't we?"

Ava nodded firmly. The last thing she wanted was for anyone to find out about the magic and take the curios away. There was so much to learn – what magic each curio contained, and what they could do with it…

"Maybe the curios' magic *should* be studied by scientists," said Sarah thoughtfully.

Ava blinked. She knew Sarah loved science but surely she didn't actually want them to tell people?

"Sarah, you're not seriously saying you want us to give up the chance to do magic, are you?" Lily said, looking at her cousin in astonishment.

A grin spread across Sarah's face as she saw Lily and Ava's shocked expressions. "No! But a scientist does need to study them though and that'll be me – starting tonight!"

Ava gave a little skip herself as she thought about the night ahead. Magic and a sleepover with her new friends – what could be better than that?

Curio House was at the top of Fentiman Street, a quiet road lined with houses and cherry trees. The huge, red-brick villa was surrounded by an overgrown walled garden on all sides. Autumn leaves were lying in huge drifts across the lawn and covered the stone steps that led up to the house.

Ava could still hardly believe she and her mum lived there. Their old house had been a cosy, two-bedroom terrace in Nottingham, while Curio House was massive, with eight bedrooms spread over the two top floors. It hadn't been decorated in years and needed a lot of work, so Ava's mum Fran was planning on doing it up slowly, starting with the rooms they used most.

When Ava opened the front door, Pepper, her Tibetan terrier, rushed towards them like a hairy black-and-white tornado, her shaggy paws skidding on the wooden floor. Sarah shrank back slightly – she was a bit anxious around dogs.

Ava crouched down. "Have you missed me, Pepper? Yes, I guess you have!" She giggled as Pepper leaped on to her lap and put her front paws on Ava's shoulder. She licked Ava's chin, her dark brown eyes shining through her long fringe. Ava kissed her. Pepper might be very naughty at times but Ava loved her to bits. When she gently pushed her off, Pepper went to say hello to Lily.

"Who's the most beautiful dog in the world? You are, aren't you, Pepper?" Lily cooed. Lily loved all animals, particularly dogs, but she wasn't allowed one because her little brother was allergic to them. After giving Lily several licks, Pepper went over to Sarah.

"Oh, um, hi, Pepper," said Sarah. She looked

alarmed as Pepper stood on her back legs and tried to reach Sarah's face with her tongue. "What's she doing?" she said nervously.

"Just saying hello. Come here, Peps," said Ava. "Sarah doesn't want your kisses."

Pepper ignored her.

"Biscuits!" called Ava.

With an excited woof, Pepper gave Sarah's chin a goodbye lick, making Sarah giggle, and then she raced to the kitchen doorway and stood there hopefully.

Ava's mum poked her head out of the dining room – the room she used as a study when she was working from home. Her chestnut hair, the same conker-brown colour as Ava's, was piled up on her head in a messy bun and she had her work clothes on. "Hi, girls. It's lovely to see you. I'm just about to take a work call though. Ava, can you get a snack for everyone?"

Ava nodded. "OK!" She led the way into the kitchen. Her mum had just finished repainting it and it looked much better than when they had first moved in. There was a large pine table in the centre of the room and an old sofa at one end, covered with a cosy blue blanket as well as a new rug on the floor.

Ava got some custard creams from the cupboard and plonked them on the table. "Here you go," she said to Lily and Sarah. Then she took a dog biscuit out of a tin for Pepper. "And this is for you."

Pepper gave Ava a look as if to say, *I'm not eating that!*

"Come on, Peps. Take the yummy biscuit!" said Ava, waggling it in front of Pepper's nose.

Pepper darted away, jumping on to the tabletop and grabbing a custard cream that had fallen out of the packet.

"Pepper!" exclaimed Ava. "I didn't mean take one of *those* biscuits!"

Eyes sparkling, Pepper took a flying leap down and in two crunches the biscuit had gone.

"Oh, Pepper! You are so naughty!" Ava said, giggling. Lily chuckled too.

"Why did she do that?" asked Sarah, looking slightly shocked.

"She doesn't think she should have to eat dog food," Ava explained. "She thinks she should have human food too, don't you, Pepper?" Pepper wagged her tail, clearly knowing she was being talked about. "It's very lucky I love you as much as I do," Ava told her.

Pepper shook herself, trotted over to Lily and looked hopefully at the custard cream in her hand.

"Nope, this is not for you," Lily told her firmly. "This is *my* food." But when Pepper continued to gaze at her she gave in, feeding her the final corner of biscuit.

Ava got them all cans of lemonade from the fridge. "OK. We've got snacks and we've got drinks. Who's ready to go and find out more about magic?"

"Me!" both Lily and Sarah exclaimed.

"Woof!" said Pepper, running to the door.

CHAPTER TWO

Ava pushed open the heavy oak door. As usual, the air in the Curio Room seemed strangely still, almost as if the room was holding its breath, waiting for something to happen.

"The ceiling's so high," said Sarah in awe as she followed Ava inside. She had only been in the Curio Room once before. She gave a shiver. "It feels kind of creepy in here."

"It feels magical," Lily breathed, her brown eyes shining as she took in the tall bookcases lining the walls and the set of shelves filled with the curios.

The rug on the floor muffled their footsteps as they went over to the curio shelves. There was a desk nearby and Pepper jumped on to the chair behind it. She turned round several times and then flopped down, her nose and paws hanging over the edge of the seat.

"You could just go and lie on the sofa where there's more room," Ava told her, pointing to the sofa at the far end of the room. But Pepper didn't move. She liked to keep an eye on what was happening.

“It’s amazing to think these things are all magic,” Lily said, studying the curios. “I wonder what they do.”

“If only there was an instruction manual,” said Sarah.

“I’ve searched the desk and there’s nothing useful in the drawers,” said Ava. “I guess we’re just going to have to figure it out for ourselves.” She joined the others, her gaze falling on the baby crocodile mummy that had come to life earlier in the week. It had charged around the streets until they had managed to catch it and send the spirit inside it back to sleep. Next to the mummy there was a metal goblet with strange carvings on and a chipped stone plaque with a mischievous-looking face that had an open mouth and vines curling from its head. Then, on the other shelves, there was a crouching stone gargoyle, dusty figurines, pieces of old jewellery, a glass bottle filled with ancient seeds, a feather fan and a brooch in the shape of a beetle, among other things.

"These books might help," said Lily, going over to the bookshelves.

"What's this?" Sarah picked up something that looked like a cross between a very small tennis racquet and a dream catcher. It had a mesh of fine wires strung across it like a spider's web and the handle was ornately carved. "*Spirit trap, Bury St Edmunds,*" she said, reading its handwritten label. "I guess it must catch spirits." She waved it around. "Do you think it works like this?"

"I have no idea," said Ava. "And why would anyone want to catch a spirit anyway?"

Sarah shrugged and read out the label of the plaque with the face on. "*Nature spirit plaque, Ledbury.*" She looked thoughtful. "It might be a good idea to catalogue the curios so we'll know if something goes missing like the crocodile did when it came to life. What do you think, Ava?"

Ava didn't really want to spend time writing things down – she found both reading and writing hard – but Sarah looked keen and it would be useful, so she nodded. "OK."

"Great!" Sarah said enthusiastically. "I'll write the notes. You read out the labels."

"Or..." Ava pulled her phone out of her pocket, "we could catalogue them this way." She started to take photos of the curios. "It's much quicker!"

Sarah grinned. "OK, that *is* faster," she admitted.

While Ava took photos, Sarah went over to the desk and picked up a box. The faded gold writing stamped into the green leather lid read: *Magyck Crystals for the Protection of the Magyck Curios.*

"The magic crystals," she breathed, opening the box.

As Ava joined her and saw the crystals glittering in the box, she felt a thrill run through her. The crystals had been the first magical thing she had discovered in Curio House. Each of the ten silk-lined compartments held a different crystal and each had their own magic power. There was also a gold necklace with a pendant, a long, thin clear crystal and a large black-and-white stone. Before Sarah had found out about the curios and joined the gang, Ava and Lily had experimented a bit with the crystals and managed to do some magic.

"It's so strange to think that these crystals are magic," said Sarah. "I mean, how is it even possible?"

"The notes written inside the lid say it's to do with their energy," said Lily, joining them.

"You can feel their energy without even touching them," Ava said. "It's weird." She ran one hand slowly over the top of the crystals and felt the air around them vibrating. Some made the air vibrate fast and others more slowly. "Here, you try, Sarah."

Sarah ran her hand over the top of the crystals

and frowned. “I don’t feel anything.”

“Try again,” Ava urged.

Sarah waved her hand over the top. “Nope, nothing.”

“Don’t worry,” Lily said. “The magic always seems to work best for Ava. I’ve been reading about crystals – normal ones, not these magic ones. People have used them for things like healing for hundreds of years. The more intuitive a person is, the easier they find it to connect with a crystal’s energy. I think Ava must be very intuitive.”

“What does that mean?” said Ava, puzzled.

“That you sense things and know stuff without having to think about it,” Lily said.

“We should do an experiment,” said Sarah eagerly. “Let’s take it in turns to hold one of the crystals and time how long it takes for the magic to work for each of us.”

Lily looked excited. “Which crystal should we use?”

"Not the Aventurine or the Amethyst," said Ava, looking at a green crystal and a purple crystal that were both duller than the rest. "I can tell their energy is really low. I think it's because we used them earlier this week. How about…" Her eyes scanned across the crystals and stopped at a white stone with black spots. "This one," she said, pointing.

Lily read out the label. "*Dalmatian Jasper: the Restorative Crystal. Dalmatian Jasper releases and restores a spirit of fun and humour, encouraging the user to bring joy to others.*"

"Sounds good!" said Sarah. "Let's set the experiment up. Ava, can you get a chair and find the stopwatch on your phone? And, Lily, can you move the other crystals out of the way just in case they can somehow affect the Jasper? I'll draw up a results table."

They followed her instructions, shooing Pepper off the chair. She went to sit by the shelves, watching them curiously. When they were ready, Ava picked the Jasper out of the box and sat down on the chair while Sarah made notes and Lily worked the stopwatch.

As soon as Ava's fingers closed round the spotty stone, a tingling spread along her hand, up her arm and throughout her whole body. She suddenly felt incredibly light and happy, like bubbles were fizzing through her blood, and a rush of laughter built up inside her. Seeing Sarah and Lily studying her, she leaped to her feet and grabbed them by the hands.

"What are you doing?" Sarah cried as Ava started to swing them both round. Pepper barked excitedly and charged around them all.

"Being happy! Life's great! It's awesome!" Seeing the shocked looks on her friends' faces, she started to laugh and found she didn't want to stop.

Letting go of their hands, Ava doubled over, laughing so much her sides hurt. Pepper bounced around her, licking her face. Tears of laughter fell down her cheeks and she rolled on to the floor. Pepper jumped on to her chest, making her laugh even more.

Suspecting she might not be able to breathe if she laughed any longer, Ava put the crystal down. The light-headed dizziness faded and her laughter gradually stopped. She lay there for a moment, getting her breath back. "Oh, wow!" she said, sitting up and wiping the tears away. "That was strange but kind of amazing! You've both got to try it."

"I'm not sure I want to," said Sarah, looking at the stone.

"You don't have to but I promise it's a nice feeling," said Ava. "And you can put the crystal down whenever you want. It's not like it's controlling you."

"I'll try next," Lily said. She handed Ava the phone to do the timing, took the Jasper Crystal and sat down. She shut her eyes. Ten seconds passed. Then twenty, and then Lily started to giggle. Her eyes blinked open and as she looked at their faces she started to giggle even more. "You both look much too serious. Cheer up! This is so much fun!" Jumping to her feet she ran to the shelf of curios, picked up the baby crocodile mummy and put on a squeaky voice.

"I'm coming to get you," she said, crouching down and making it dance across the floor towards them. "I'm going to gobble you up!"

"Lily, what are you doing?" said Sarah, half shocked, half amused.

"Put the crocodile down, Lily," said Ava, grinning.

"But I'm enjoying myself. I'm a mummy and I'm coming to get you!" said Lily, giggling and waving the crocodile in their faces. "RAAARRRR!"

Ava grabbed it off her. "Give me that!"

"Meanie spoilsport," said Lily, pouting like a two-year-old.

Ava started to grin. Her friend really did look like she was having fun. Lily's eyes lit up and she ran over to the shelves again. Grabbing the stone plaque with the carved face on, she crouched down behind the desk with it.

Ava and Sarah looked at each other.

"What are you doing now?" Sarah called.

"You'll have to come and see," said Lily in a sing-song voice.

They walked cautiously over.

"BOO!" shouted Lily, holding the plaque in front of her face and jumping out from behind the desk. They both leaped back and she collapsed on the floor laughing, clutching the plaque.

Pepper barked loudly. For a moment, Ava thought she saw a flicker of green light flash across the room but before she had time to mention it to the others, the door opened and her mum looked in.

"Whatever are you up to in here, girls?" she exclaimed.

CHAPTER THREE

"Nothing, Mum!" gasped Ava, grabbing Pepper and trying to make her be quiet.

"Sorry for making so much noise," said Sarah.

Ava's mum peered at Lily, who was lying on the floor, hiding the crystal and plaque in her arms and trying so hard not to laugh she looked like she was about to burst. "Are you OK, Lily?"

"Yes! I'm fine!" squeaked Lily.

"We'll keep the noise down, Mum," said Ava, desperate for her mum to leave. "Promise!"

"OK. I'm glad you're having fun," her mum

said and she left them to it.

Lily instantly exploded into gales of laughter. "That was so funny!"

"Imagine what Mum would say if she knew we were doing magic," said Ava.

Lily put the crystal on the desk and then placed the plaque safely back on the top shelf. She blinked as the effects of the magic faded. "Gosh. That was brilliant."

"OK, I guess it's my turn," said Sarah, slightly nervously.

"You really don't have to," said Ava.

"No, I want to, it looks fun," said Sarah. "And it will be good to have my reactions for the results table. Ava, will you time how long it takes for me to be affected by the magic? Lily, can you write down what I do?"

"Sure, and don't worry, you'll be fine," Lily reassured her. "You'll probably just laugh a lot and you can put the crystal down if you don't like it."

Sarah took the crystal and sat down. Nothing happened. "What do I do?" she said, looking at Ava. "How do I make it work?"

"I don't know," said Ava. "The magic just happens for me."

"It doesn't for me," said Lily. "Try shutting your eyes, focus on the crystal and let your mind open like a flower ready to let the magic in."

"What kind of flower?" asked Sarah earnestly.

"I don't know, just a flower," said Lily.

"But flowers are all so different," said Sarah, frowning. "Should I be imagining a daffodil or a rose or a bluebell..."

"Sarah! Just imagine any flower," said Ava impatiently. She saw Sarah open her mouth again. "OK, think of a red rose. Is that better? Can you picture it now?"

Sarah nodded. "I guess, but is it a standard rose or a miniature rose or a—"

"Sarah!" both Ava and Lily groaned.

Sarah shut her eyes. After a minute, she shook her head. "Nope, it's no good. I'm still not feeling any different. I think the rose image isn't working for me. Maybe I should think about the particles of gas spreading out when you put them in a container..." She broke off, a smile catching at her mouth. "Wait, I've just thought of a really funny joke." She looked at them. "So, I was reading a book on helium and guess what?"

"What?" said Ava.

"I couldn't put it down!" Sarah burst out laughing.

Ava and Lily exchanged confused looks.

Sarah saw their faces. "Helium? It's a gas that's lighter than air. I couldn't put the book down? Do you get it now?" She shook her head. "Fine, how about this one? Why can you never trust atoms?"

"Why?" said Lily.

"They make up everything!" said Sarah, giggling. "Oh, come on, guys – laugh!" she said when they both looked blank. "Everything's made of atoms, that's why it's funny!" They both started to smile, not at the joke but at Sarah's enthusiasm. "Well, if you don't like science jokes how about a maths joke?" she went on. "What did one prime number say to—"

Ava plucked the stone out of Sarah's hand and plonked it back in the box. Maths jokes were definitely a step too far!

Sarah blinked several times. "Wow! I really wanted to make you smile and all these science jokes just started coming into my head."

"I felt like that too," said Lily. "Only I didn't get science jokes in my head."

"I just felt really happy, so happy I couldn't stop laughing," said Ava.

Sarah looked thoughtful. "Maybe we should try to learn how to control the magic more so we can use it to do stuff rather than just having a laugh. There's so much we need to find out, like why does the Jasper work quicker for Ava than Lily and for Lily than me? Is it really because of intuition? And why does the same stone affect us in different ways? Will all the stones do that? Hmm." Her eyes fell on the box. "How about we try another one?" She picked up a glossy black crystal. "*Obsidian*," she read out. *"The Seeing Crystal. Obsidian enhances the ability to see that which is elsewhere and to see those things that go unseen by many."*

She handed it to Ava and picked up a pen. "Now how do you feel?"

Ava looked around. "It's not making me see any better." As her own energy connected to the crystal's energy, the world seemed to go blurry, as if the room had suddenly filled with a fine fog. She looked around again, puzzled.

"If anything it's making my sight worse."
She noticed Pepper sniffing and scratching at the wall beside the desk and then blinked. The desk seemed to be glowing with a golden light. Going closer, she saw that it wasn't the whole desk that was glowing but a small, circular spot just below the brass handle of the central drawer beneath the desktop. The closer she got the stronger the glow became.

"What are you doing?" said Lily.

"I can see something." Ava felt the glowing spot. She caught her breath as she realized it was a hidden button! She pressed it and another drawer slid smoothly out of the bottom of the main, central drawer.

"It's a secret drawer!" gasped Sarah.

Ava pulled out a well-used notebook. "And look what's inside!" There were drawings and crossings-out, some pages seemed to be written in code and others had been torn out. The writing was small and cramped.

"Lily, what does it say?" Ava asked. She wasn't great at reading but Lily could read faster than anyone Ava had ever met!

Lily's gaze swept over the pages. "It's full of notes about the curios – and the crystals too, by the look of it."

Just then, Pepper woofed and ran to the door.

From the hall, they could hear the front door opening and the sound of voices.

"I bet that's our mums," said Lily. "They said they'd drop round our sleeping stuff."

Ava's mum looked into the Curio Room. "Girls, your mums are here. Do you want to come and get your bags?"

Ava felt a stab of frustration. The last thing she wanted to do was leave the Curio Room but there was nothing for it. "Sure," she said to her mum. "We'll come back to this later," she whispered to the others.

Ava's mum had shown Sarah and Lily's mums into the lounge. It was one of the many rooms that hadn't been redecorated yet. Great-Aunt Enid's faded sofas were hard and uncomfortable, the rug on the floor was threadbare and the mantelpiece was covered with a layer of dust. Lily's mum Cai was wearing sports leggings and a fleece, and was admiring the fireplace. Sarah's mum Ruth sat on the edge of one of the sofas, her hands folded in her lap. *Everything about her looks polished*, Ava thought, noticing her perfectly painted nails, her shiny brown hair and her small, glossy handbag that was beside her on the sofa.

"Please excuse the state of the place," said Ava's mum. "We've got so much to do still."

"It's an incredible house," said Lily's mum, looking around. "It's going to be absolutely wonderful when you've done it up, Fran."

"Thank you," said Ava's mum, smiling. "We're going to have to live in chaos for a few years though."

Ruth laughed. "I wish I was more like you. When we moved from Australia last year, I had to get everything sorted straight away. I hate it when things are out of place."

Ava's mum smiled. "Luckily Ava and I don't mind too much. Now, can I get you both a cup of tea or coffee? It's really nice to finally meet you, Ruth." She'd already met Cai earlier in the week.

"And you," Ruth said politely. "Sarah has told me all about Ava." The look she gave Ava suggested she didn't completely like what she'd heard. Ava thought she knew why. At the start of the week, Sarah had been unhappy about Lily and Ava becoming friends, worrying she would lose her best friend. Now Sarah knew about the curios and had got to know Ava, it was all fine between them. But maybe Sarah's mum didn't realize that.

"I don't think your mum likes me very much," Ava whispered to Sarah as they went to the kitchen to help bring things through.

Sarah looked embarrassed. "Sorry. It's probably because I was unhappy when you and Lily first became friends but I'm sure she'll soon change her mind."

Ava gave her a reassuring grin. "Don't worry. I'll try to win her over."

"Arghhhhh!" Hearing a high-pitched scream, the girls exchanged alarmed looks and raced back into the lounge.

CHAPTER FOUR

Sarah's mum was standing up, looking shocked. Pepper was balancing on the back of the sofa – her tail wagging, her pink tongue hanging out.

"Your dog!" Ruth spluttered. "It just leaped up on to the back of the sofa behind me and licked my cheek!"

"I'm so sorry," said Ava's mum, who had run in after the girls, a plate of biscuits in her hand. "Pepper does like to jump on to high places."

"She's a real cutie," said Cai, chuckling as Pepper looked at them through her fringe.

"Cute but naughty," said Ava's mum, lifting Pepper down. "Please do sit down again, Ruth. I'll put Pepper in the kitchen if she's bothering you and—"

"Pepper! No!" gasped Ava, seeing Pepper sniffing Ruth's little handbag and realizing what she was about to do. Pepper grabbed the bag and bounded away.

"My handbag!" cried Ruth.

Lily grabbed a cookie from the plate. "Biscuits! Here, Pepper!"

Pepper instantly dropped the bag and ran to Lily. Ava fetched it. "I'm really sorry," she apologized to Ruth. "Here it is." Ruth grimaced slightly as she touched the bag that was damp from being in Pepper's mouth.

Scooping Pepper up, Ava's mum carried her out to the kitchen but Pepper was not amused at being shut away and she barked loudly and scrabbled at the kitchen door with her claws.

Ava's mum came back. She, Cai and Ruth chatted for a while and then Cai asked the girls what they were planning on doing the next day.

"We're going to walk into town and have a look round the shops," said Ava.

"You're not going on your own, are you?" said Ruth, sounding worried. "I don't think you're old enough for that."

"Mum!" Sarah hissed.

"Sarah, you're only ten," her mum said.

"I'm sure the girls will be fine, Ruth," Cai said. "Eastwold is very safe and it's only a short walk from here."

"I'm sorry, but I'm really not happy about Sarah going into town without an adult," said Ruth. "If Lily and Ava are going to do that then I'll pick Sarah up first thing."

Ava saw her mum glance at Sarah who had gone pink with embarrassment. "There's really no need. I can walk into town with the girls."

Ruth smiled. "Thanks, Fran. In that case, Sarah, I'll pick you up as planned." A few minutes later she left, picking dog hairs off her coat as she went.

As the girls carried their bags upstairs to Ava's room, Sarah sighed. "I wish my mum didn't worry so much. I'm not a baby but she still treats me like one. She's only just let me have a phone and I'm not allowed to go on social media at all."

Ava gave her a sympathetic look. Her own mum was very relaxed about most things – mobile phones, bedtimes. It had been just the two of them since her mum and dad had got divorced five years ago and she sometimes felt that her mum was more like a sister.

"At least you've got a mobile phone now," she said.

"Yes, though Mum sometimes checks my messages," said Sarah. She lowered her voice.

"So make sure you never mention magic if you text me."

Ava nodded and led the way into her room. They made up their beds using the blow-up mattresses that Ava's mum had got out and then played a game Ava made up which involved them running round the two landings and throwing Ava's beanie toys at each other, scoring points for the number of times they hit someone. The game only ended when Pepper ran off with all the Beanie Babies!

After a yummy tea of home-made pizza and ice cream they got into their pyjamas and fetched the leather notebook from the Curio Room, taking it upstairs to read. Ava really wanted to find out what Great-Aunt Enid had written but, as usual when she tried to read, the words were just a jumble of letters that didn't make sense and seemed to move around. Lily had already finished the whole of the first page by the time Ava had managed to figure out that the underlined words at the top of the page said, *Notes About the Crystals of Protection.*

"Hang on, Lily, I haven't finished yet!" said Sarah as Lily started to turn the page, which made Ava feel a bit better.

"Sorry," said Lily, turning it back.

"You're so fast at reading – why don't you read it and tell us what it says?" said Sarah.

Lily nodded eagerly. "OK!"

While she read, Ava and Sarah sorted out the midnight feast. Ava's mum had got them little bags of jelly sweets as well as some popcorn, Lily had brought a large bar of chocolate and Sarah's mum had dropped off a punnet of juicy strawberries. Ava and Sarah divided everything between three bowls.

"Are we really going to stay up until midnight?" Sarah asked. "When Lily and I sleepover at each other's our mums usually make us have a midnight feast early. We're never allowed to stay up till actual midnight."

"Well, we can tonight. We'll just pretend to go to sleep when Mum comes in," said Ava. "She'll only check once."

Sarah beamed. "Cool! So, what shall we do now?"

"We could play badminton," suggested Ava. "Mum and I did that the other night. She found some old badminton racquets while she was clearing out one of the rooms. The upstairs landing's perfect for it. Do you want to play too, Lily?"

Lily shook her head. Pepper had curled up beside her on the bed. "I'm fine here," she said, stroking Pepper with one hand and turning the pages with the other. "This bit is all about how your aunt was given the crystals when she visited Egypt and her thoughts on how they work. I'll tell you everything I find out."

"Brilliant!" said Ava. Lily doing all the reading suited her just fine!

Ava and Sarah went up to the next floor where there was a long, wide landing with rooms opening off it. There was no carpet on the bare floorboards, just piles of things that Ava's mum had started sorting into heaps.

After they had played badminton for a while, Ava spotted a massive old dog bed and had another idea. "Let's slide down the stairs on this!"

The stairs leading from the top floor to the middle floor were straight. Ava piled some old curtains at the bottom and then she and Sarah took it in turns to sit on the dog bed and slide down the stairs, landing in the soft pile of curtains.

At first Sarah was cautious and bumped down slowly step by step, using her feet to stop herself going too fast, but after a few goes she started to let herself go faster and soon she was flying down almost as quickly as Ava.

Hearing the thuds, Pepper trotted out of Ava's bedroom to see what they were doing. When it was Ava's go, Pepper leaped on the dog bed with her. Ava grinned. "OK, you can have a turn too!"

Sarah gave them a huge push. The dog bed bumped down the staircase with Pepper woofing excitedly.

"I've found something out!" Lily said, running out of

the bedroom waving the notebook. She broke off with a squeal as Ava and Pepper hit the pile of curtains and flew off, Ava rolling into her legs and almost knocking her over.

Ava scrambled to her feet. "What is it?" she asked, seeing the excitement on Lily's face.

"It's something really important about the crystals!" said Lily, her eyes glowing. "Quick! Come with me!"

CHAPTER FIVE

They all piled into Ava's room, Pepper leaping on to the bed and sitting bolt upright. She was just as keen to hear what Lily had found out as Sarah and Ava.

"Well?" Ava said impatiently.

"I've found out how to recharge the crystals!" Lily said.

"Great," said Ava.

"How do we do it?" asked Sarah eagerly.

Lily quickly explained. "The long, thin crystal in the box is called a Selenite wand. Selenite is a very powerful cleansing crystal that can –" she checked the notebook – "*absorb negative energy and recharge positive energy.*"

"How do we make it work?" asked Ava.

"The notes say we touch it to the crystal that needs recharging and hold it there for a minute. You can do it at any time but it works best if you do it in moonlight." Lily read out, "*Moonlight activates all magical energy, particularly that of stones and crystals. The crystals of protection will be at their strongest when they are bathed in the light of a full moon.* There's an arrow and extra note here as well. *N.B.*"

"That basically means take note," Sarah added.

Lily nodded. "*N.B. Be very careful where the curios are positioned!*" She frowned. "I have no idea what that means. Why should it matter where the curios are?"

"I don't know," said Ava, jumping to her feet. "But let's not worry about that now." She pointed to her window where a full moon was glowing like a white ball in the evening sky. "Let's get recharging the crystals!"

Just then the door opened and Ava's mum looked in. "Time to settle down now, girls, though I'm not sure how much you'll sleep with Pepper snoring beside you!"

"She doesn't snore … much," Ava said. "Night, Mum."

"Night, all of you," said her mum as they got into their beds and snuggled down. "Sleep well."

But Ava had absolutely no intention of going to sleep just yet. As soon as her mum had turned the light off and left, Ava switched on her torch and they all sat back up. "We'll wait for my mum to go to sleep and then we'll go to the Curio Room," she whispered.

The others nodded excitedly.

While they waited, they took it in turns to point the torch up at their faces and tell ghost stories. Ava's were definitely the scariest! Sarah ended up covering her ears.

"And then the boy turned the light off and icy-cold fingers touched his neck and he heard a creepy voice saying—" Ava broke off with a yelp as Lily threw pillows at her. "Don't you like my story?" she said, acting hurt.

"No!" said Lily. "Let's watch funny cat videos on my phone instead."

"OK," sighed Ava, although she was actually quite relieved because she had been making the story up and she wasn't sure how it was going to end.

After a while, Ava tiptoed out on to the landing. There was no light coming from under her mum's door and she had switched off her music. "Time to go!" she whispered.

Trying not to giggle with excitement, they crept downstairs with Pepper. The moonlight was shining in through the tall windows of the Curio Room, lighting up the shelf of curios and causing a pattern of tiger stripes to appear on the floor.

The air felt even more still and silent than it usually did. Pepper gave an uneasy growl.

"Shhh," Ava told her. She turned to the others. "Let's not put the lights on, just in case Mum comes downstairs." Although her mum wasn't strict, Ava knew she wouldn't be happy if she found them creeping around the house after she'd told them to go to sleep.

Pepper ran over to the shelves and prowled around. Ava went to the desk and took the Aventurine and Amethyst crystals out of the box. Carrying them over to a nearby window ledge, she placed them in the moonlight. Then she fetched the long, thin piece of Selenite. "Here goes," she said, touching the end of the Selenite wand to the dull purple Amethyst.

"I'll time you for sixty seconds," said Sarah.

For a few seconds nothing happened but then suddenly a spark lit up in the centre of the crystal. It flickered and then grew stronger and brighter, growing and expanding until the whole crystal was glittering with a wild purple light.

"Oh, wow!" breathed Ava.

"Sixty seconds is up," said Sarah.

Ava took the Selenite away and the light faded to a gentle glow. She passed her hand over the top and felt the crystal now vibrating with fresh energy. Her palm tingled and she beamed. "It worked!"

Next, she used the Selenite on the Aventurine and the same thing happened. She looked with delight at the two glowing crystals. "Awesome! They're both recharged, which means we can use them again. And now we know what to do whenever a crystal runs out of power." She went to pick them up but Lily got there first. "I'll put them back in the box. The crystals work so quickly for you and we really don't want that now. It's late and your mum could come in at any moment."

Ava felt a flash of disappointment. "OK," she said reluctantly. "We won't do any more magic until tomorrow."

Sarah shut the box and they headed out of the room. At the door, Ava stopped. "Pepper! Come on!"

Pepper was sniffing the wall beside the desk, ignoring her, so Ava went back and scooped her up. "Bedtime," she said. But as she straightened up, she paused. There was something about the curios that seemed different. What was it? She scanned the shelves. Something niggled her, catching at her mind like a splinter in a finger, but she couldn't work out what it was.

"Ava, come on!" urged Lily.

With one last puzzled look at the shelves, Ava hurried after the others.

CHAPTER SIX

Ava, Lily and Sarah managed to stay up until midnight by discussing what they would like to do with the crystals. Sarah wanted to try the Healing Crystal, Lily liked the idea of trying out the Dream Crystal and Ava wanted to have another go with the Manifestation Crystal, which could make things you desired appear.

Pepper helped keep them awake. She kept jumping up on the window seat and staring down into the garden, occasionally bursting into a flurry of short, sharp barks that made the girls jump.

"Why is she doing that?" asked Sarah.

"She can probably hear things in the garden," said Ava. Outside an owl hooted and Pepper barked again. "Pepper, be quiet!" she said, going over and taking her off the window seat. "It's just an owl. Come and sit with me."

"It's almost midnight," yawned Lily. "Should we start the midnight feast?"

The midnight feast distracted Pepper. She went round all three girls, staring at them beseechingly until they each gave her some popcorn.

Lily giggled as Pepper pawed her arm for more. "Pepper! It's popcorn not PUPcorn!"

"And it's really not GRRRReat for your teeth," Ava told her, scooping her up and kissing her.

Putting the unfinished sweets, strawberries and popcorn on the desk out of Pepper's reach, they got back into their beds and this time cuddled down for real. Pepper lay at the end of Ava's bed.

"Night, everyone," Ava said.

"Night," whispered Lily sleepily.

Sarah was already asleep.

Ava felt Pepper start to get up. "Oh no, you don't," she said, pulling the terrier into her arms. "You're not barking at the window all night, no matter how many owls you hear out there!" Pepper tensed as if she was going to struggle but then gave in and flopped against Ava, lifting her head back so she could lick her cheek. Ava snuggled down with Pepper in her arms and soon they were both fast asleep.

✦

Ava was the first to wake up in the morning. She jumped out of bed and threw open the curtains. The others sat up sleepily, rubbing their eyes as the light fell on them.

It was a sunny day outside. Ava opened the window, breathing in the damp scent of fallen autumn leaves. The sun was rising in the sky, shining down on the trees and the overgrown garden. *It is* really *overgrown,* Ava thought, looking at the creepers that were scrambling over the wall and the long green grass coated with dew. Patches of nettles clustered around the tree trunks. Weeds were sprouting through the cracks in the paving slabs and bramble bushes seemed to have grown up overnight. Pepper ran to Ava's bedroom door and scratched at it.

"I'm just going to let Pepper out," Ava said as the other two started to sit up. "See you downstairs!"

She pulled on her dressing gown and hurried to the kitchen. As soon as she opened the door, Pepper raced outside. Mum was getting breakfast ready, her hair pulled back in a scrunchy. "How did you all sleep?" she asked.

"Fine," said Ava. She looked out of the window. Pepper was running across the grass, her nose to the ground as if she was following a scent. "What's she doing?" she said.

Ava's mum watched Pepper for a moment. "Maybe there was a fox in the garden last night." She shook her head. "We'd better do some gardening this afternoon. I can't believe it's growing so fast. Will you give me a hand?"

"Sure," said Ava. She quite liked gardening. "Can we still go into town this morning though?"

Her mum nodded. "What do you want to do?"

"Just have a look round," said Ava. They'd been so busy since they moved in that she'd hardly had a chance to explore the town and she really wanted to. It was a very old market town with narrow, cobbled streets. "Lily said she'd show me her favourite places – there's a sweet shop and a cookie shop, a stationery shop and a shop that sells models of fairies and dragons!"

"Fun! How about we all walk in together, then you can leave me in a coffee shop and come and find me when you're done. Does that sound OK?"

Ava beamed. "It sounds perfect," she said.

✦

The sun shone as they walked into town along the river. Despite it being autumn and the leaves having fallen from the trees, everywhere looked surprisingly fresh and green. The grass was thick and lush. The reeds beside the riverbank were tall and thick, and the roses in the flower beds seemed to have had a new lease of life. As they crossed the footbridge into town they passed a house with a front garden full of enormous yellow sunflowers. A boy was staring up at them with his dad. Ava's mum sneezed a few times and stopped to find a tissue in her bag. Ava recognized the boy from school and called to him.

"Hey, Jack, your sunflowers are massive!"

Jack looked round. "It's really weird. They grew taller overnight. I can't wait to show Fin – his grandad gave us the seeds and we're having a competition to see who can grow the biggest ones."

"You're definitely going to win," said Lily, looking at the huge sunflowers.

"I don't think I've ever seen sunflowers so big," said Sarah, nodding.

Ava's mum sneezed again. "Oh dear. It feels

like my hayfever's starting up but surely it can't be at this time of year."

"I don't know. My eyes have been really itchy. There must be pollen in the air," said Jack's dad.

"Probably because the weather's so mild," said Ava's mum.

"That's global warming for you," sighed Jack's dad.

Ava noticed two worms wriggling across the pavement in the sunshine and nudged Lily and Sarah. "What do you call it when worms take over the world?"

"What?" said Lily.

Ava grinned. "Global WORMING!" Lily and Sarah giggled and, saying goodbye to Jack and his dad, they all walked on. Everywhere Ava looked she saw plants growing – flowers blooming in window boxes and weeds pushing up through the tiniest cracks.

They reached the square in the middle of the town. There was a fountain in the centre and a café with outside tables and patio heaters. A network of cobbled streets led off in all directions.

"I'll get myself a coffee," said Ava's mum, nodding at the café. "And you three can have a wander round."

It was great fun being able to explore the town on their own. Lily showed them the shops she liked best and told them what she knew about the town's history. "The shops and houses were built in the Middle Ages," she explained. "Eastwold was one of the most important towns in the country back then. There are secret tunnels under the town and all sorts of old objects have been dug up when areas of the town have been excavated. In the 1500s it was known as the centre of magic – people used to come here to get spells or be healed."

"Cool!" said Ava.

"Why did people think it was so magical?" asked Sarah.

"It's to do with ley lines," said Lily. "There are some people who think that if you draw imaginary straight lines between ancient landmarks, the places where the lines cross attract magic. Eastwold has loads of ley lines crossing it."

"But ley lines aren't real," said Sarah sceptically. "There's no scientific proof for them."

"People say magic isn't real," Ava pointed out. "But we know different."

Sarah grinned. "I guess you're right. Maybe ley lines do exist too."

Ava loved the idea that they lived somewhere that attracted magic. "I wonder if Great-Aunt Enid chose to live here because it's so magical?"

"She does say something about that in her notebook," said Lily. "She says magic attracts magic, which must be why magic objects often seem to end up in Eastwold. I think she collected quite a few of the curios from antique shops around here."

"What else did you find out about the curios?" asked Sarah.

"There seem to be two different types. There are curios that can do things, like a curse cup, a mirror that shows the future, and divining rods that can find precious things. Then there are curios that have magical spirits inside them. The spirits can be woken up, just like the crocodile spirit was by the Osiris Stone – the big black-and-white stone in the crystal box."

"Is it only the Osiris Stone that can wake them up?" asked Sarah.

"No, the notes mention curios being woken up by magical water, moonlight and flowers, and some can be woken up by reading out the words written on them."

"We really do need to find out more," said Sarah. "We don't want to accidentally wake up a spirit again!"

"Agreed," said Ava. Her eyes fell on a shop that had a window full of enormous meringues swirled with raspberry ripples, and chocolate brownies in all different flavours. "But now

I think it's time we did some magic of our own."

"What do you mean?" Sarah asked.

"We're going to make three of those brownies disappear," said Ava.

Sarah looked intrigued. "How?"

Ava pulled her purse out of her pocket and grinned. "By buying and eating them!"

✦

They were walking down the street, munching on the delicious gooey brownies, when a familiar figure came out of a clothes shop.

"Mum!" said Sarah in surprise.

Her mum stopped. "Sarah! What are you doing in town on your own?"

"We're not on our own," said Ava quickly. "My mum's at the café in the square."

"If she's not with you, it means you're on your own," said Sarah's mum.

"Not really," Ava pointed out. "Mum is here in town with us but—"

"Please don't argue, Ava." Ruth turned to Sarah. "Sarah, I'm very disappointed. I told you that I didn't want you here without an adult."

"But, Mum, we're not—"

"No, Sarah," her mother interrupted. "You've deliberately gone against my wishes, which only proves I was right in thinking that you're not old enough to be allowed into town on your own."

"We won't do it again, Auntie Ruth," said Lily.

"You're right, you won't," said Sarah's mum crisply. "Ava, take me to your mother, please."

CHAPTER SEVEN

Ava led the way back to the square. Sarah looked completely mortified. "*Sorry*," Ava mouthed at her, feeling bad that Sarah was in trouble. She really hadn't thought Sarah's mum would mind them going off for a little while and she was sure it hadn't crossed her mum's mind either. When they reached the café, Ava saw her mum's surprise as Sarah's mum marched towards her and knew she was right.

"I'm so sorry," Ava's mum apologized when Sarah's mum told her how upset she was at finding the girls walking through town on their own. "I didn't think it would be a problem. Isn't it good for them to have a little independence?"

"They're too young," said Ruth firmly. "I'll take Sarah home with me now and pick her things up later. Sarah, what do you say?"

"Thank you for having me to stay," Sarah muttered, her cheeks burning.

"That's no problem, sweetie. You can come again, any time," said Ava's mum.

Looking at Ruth's cross face, Ava didn't think that would be happening soon.

Ruth and Sarah left and Ava and Lily sat down at the table with Ava's mum. "Oh dear. I probably should have realized Ruth wouldn't want you going off on your own, even for a little while."

"Auntie Ruth worries about all kinds of stuff," said Lily. "It's not just Sarah being out on her own. She didn't like it when my mum let us have Coca-Cola the first time Sarah stayed over after they moved back here from Australia, because she doesn't like Sarah to have caffeine, and then another time she was upset when Mum let us watch a movie that was rated a twelve."

"I'm glad you're not that strict, Mum," said Ava, picking up a salt cellar and playing with it.

"Every parent's different, Ava," her mum said. "Sarah is a year younger than you two, after all, and if Ruth worries then we need to make sure we try to respect her wishes from now on. It'll only be because she wants to protect her daughter."

"My mum says she thinks Auntie Ruth worries about Sarah being out on her own partly because in Australia there are so many dangerous things – spiders, snakes..."

"Crocodiles," Ava put in, sending Lily a grin as she remembered how Sarah's knowledge of crocodiles had come in really handy on their last adventure.

"Crocodiles," Lily agreed, grinning back.

Ava got to her feet and went round the table to hug her mum. "I'm very glad I've got you as my mum!" Her mum hugged her back.

"Now how about I get you both a drink and then we'll pick up some sandwiches for lunch?" Her hazel eyes twinkled and she suddenly looked just like Ava. "Coca-Cola, Lily?"

Lily chuckled. "Yes, please!"

+

On the way home, Ava and Lily were walking up Fentiman Road when they saw two of Ava's elderly neighbours chatting – Bob and Albert. They were standing on their drive and Bob was holding a very large pumpkin.

"Look at it!" he was saying. "Last night it was the size of a tennis ball – I was going to chuck it on the compost heap today – but when I got to the allotment, I found it had grown into this!" He held the pumpkin up. "How did that happen?"

"Well, I don't rightly know," said Albert. "And look at my geraniums." He nodded to the pots of red and white flowers on either side of their front door. The flowers were spilling out in abundance. "Yesterday they were as good as dead and today, well, look at them. They've gone wild."

"We're certainly enjoying a last burst of summer," said Ava's mum, stopping. "My garden's turned into a jungle."

Ava sighed. Not another conversation about gardening and the weather!

"I've never known anything like it," said Bob. "And it's not just the pumpkins. Our runner beans have produced another crop this morning too. In November!"

"It's like magic," said Albert, shaking his head.

Ava caught her breath, feeling like a jolt of electricity had just shot through her. *Magic!* While her mum continued to chat with the men, she pulled Lily's arm. "Quick! Come with me!"

Lily followed her into the garden of Curio House. "What is it?"

Ava swept her arm around the garden, walls of yellow and white flowers poking their heads out between the brambles. "All these plants... Did you hear what Albert said? Do you think it could be happening because of magic?"

"Magic?" echoed Lily, her eyes widening.

"Maybe one of the curios has made the plants grow," said Ava.

They raced to the Curio Room, letting Pepper out of the kitchen on the way. When they got there, Ava counted the curios and frowned.

"They are all still here," she said. She cast her eyes over the shelves, checking against the photos she'd taken – top shelf, middle shelves, bottom shelf... "Nothing's moved. Everything's in the exactly same position as it was before."

She felt half relieved and half disappointed. She was glad a curio hadn't come to life again and escaped like the crocodile, of course, but at the same time it would have been quite fun to try to capture it.

"It must be global warming after all," said Lily, looking out of the window at the overgrown garden.

"Now we're here, maybe we could do some magic?" Ava said, looking at the crystals.

"We should probably wait until Sarah's with us," Lily pointed out.

Ava nodded. "You're right. I hope she's OK. Should I text her?" Lily nodded so Ava sent a text.

Are u ok??? Do u want to meet up tomorrow? We can do some more science experiments...

She added a winking face, remembering Sarah had warned them her mum sometimes checked her messages so they must never mention magic.

They waited but Sarah didn't reply.

"Auntie Ruth's probably taken her phone away," said Lily. "Why don't you come to mine in the morning and we'll ask if Sarah can come out then?"

"Great," said Ava. "And if she does, we can try out the Amethyst."

"Just don't start thinking about dog food like the last time you used it," Lily said.

"Or dogs," said Ava. "Imagine dogs raining down from the sky!"

"Let's not," said Lily with a grin.

+

After lunch, Lily's dad came to collect her, and Ava and her mum set about trying to tidy up the garden. Ava's mum gave Ava a large spray bottle of saltwater to get rid of the weeds on the patio – weeds hated salt. Ava started spraying every weed she could see but there were so many, it was hard work. Looking round at the green sea of vegetation and the flowers, she couldn't help wondering again if magic had something to do with it. It was just so odd.

She glanced at the Curio Room windows

as she started to plant some bulbs in pots. She'd checked the photos against the shelves and the curios were all where they should be. So why did she feel something wasn't right?

"Ava, sweetie! You're planting those bulbs upside down!" her mum exclaimed.

"Whoops! Sorry!" Ava said. Pushing thoughts of the curios out of her mind, she fished the bulbs out of the soil and started again.

+

When Ava woke the next morning, she threw open her curtains. The sight made her stare. The plants in the garden had grown again overnight! Trumpet vines were now spreading across the lawn, blooming with white flowers. The trees were sprouting green buds on their bare branches, fresh roses were scrambling over the garden walls, the bulbs she had planted were already poking shoots out through the compost in the pots and the weeds she had got rid of had regrown.

It's impossible, Ava thought, her heart somersaulting. *Bulbs and plants don't grow this quickly even when it's warm. It* has *to be magic!*

She ran downstairs to the Curio Room. On the top shelf she could see the stone gargoyle, the spirit trap, the brass cup, the stone plaque and the crocodile mummy. Below that were the figurines and jewellery, the bottle with seeds in, divining rods, a hair comb and mirror…

Nothing had moved but she had the definite feeling that something had changed from the other day. It was like doing a spot the difference puzzle. She was usually very good at them. She frowned as she looked at all the objects but she couldn't work it out.

Still puzzling over it, she went into the kitchen. Her mum was in there, sneezing loudly. "Goodness, my hayfever's bad again today," she said, wiping her streaming eyes. "And look –" she pointed to the window where a honeybee was trying to get out – "the weather is so warm it's woken up the bees! I've never known anything like it!"

Ava went to the window and let the bee out. As it flew off towards the roses, she frowned. She was sure something magical was going on – but what?

✦

After breakfast, Ava set off to Lily's house with Pepper. Across the road, Albert and Bob's geraniums were bursting out of their pots in a riot of red and white, and the grass on the verges and people's front lawns had grown from a few centimetres to knee high.

Lily came hurrying out as soon as she saw Ava coming up her drive. "Something magic's definitely going on," she said, patting Pepper who was jumping up and down in excitement at seeing her.

Ava nodded. "Plants just don't go wild and grow like this, especially not in November." She grinned. "It's a mys-TREE!"

"Ha ha," said Lily, rolling her eyes. "Come on, let's get Sarah," she said, looking at the climbing frame in her garden that was now covered with ivy. "Then we can try to get to the ROOT of the problem!"

They both giggled.

On the way to Sarah's house, they passed

the allotments. People were exclaiming over their huge marrows, courgettes and pumpkins, and a sea of poppies was now blooming between the vegetable patches.

When they reached Sarah's house, her mum answered the door.

"Hi, Auntie Ruth," said Lily. "Can Sarah come out?"

Sarah's mum's eyes swept to Ava and Pepper. "Not today."

"Just for a little while?" Ava asked hopefully.

"No," said Sarah's mum. "I'm sorry, girls. You'll be able to see each other tomorrow at school."

She shut the door. Ava and Lily looked at each other in frustration but there was nothing they could do.

✦

"OK, so all the curios are definitely here and none of them has moved?" Lily checked as they arrived back at Ava's house and went straight to the Curio Room.

Ava nodded, looking along the shelves and feeling a memory trying to swim up to the surface of her mind. Her gaze stopped on the top shelf, her instincts telling her that something was wrong there. She was sure something looked different but what was it…?

"The stone plaque," she gasped as she suddenly realized what had been bothering her. "Lily! The face carved into it has gone!"

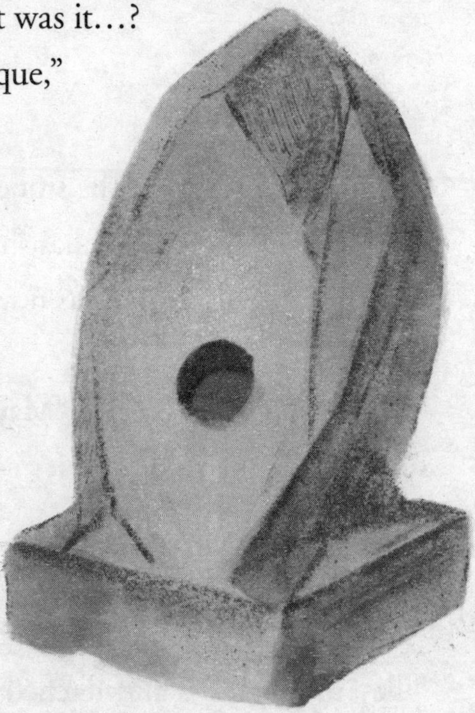

CHAPTER EIGHT

Lily and Ava stared at the stone plaque. The face with the vines instead of hair had disappeared and the ancient plaque was now just smooth stone.

Lily caught her breath. "Maybe there was a spirit inside the stone and it's escaped!"

"How?" exclaimed Ava.

"The notebook might say," said Lily. "I'm sure I read something about the plaque." They ran upstairs and fetched the notebook. Lily's eyes skimmed the pages. "Crystals…

Curios… The kind of magic they have… How the magic can be released and … yes! Here it is!" She fell silent as she turned the pages, reading the notes. "Oh… OH!"

"What is it?" demanded Ava.

Lily read out. *"The twelfth-century stone plaque contains a nature spirit. Nature spirits are mischievous spirits of positive energy that are attracted to areas where things grow. If released, the spirit will cause nature to run rampant. Plants will grow and flowers will bloom, no matter the season. It will continue until the spirit returns to the stone and is sent back to sleep."*

"So, there's a nature spirit on the loose," said Ava, trying to take it in. "But how did it wake up and get out of the plaque?"

"I read something about that too." Lily flicked back through the notes and then stabbed a finger down. *"If a spirit is awakened it may escape out of the curio using a conduit."*

"What's a conduit?" said Ava.

Lily shrugged.

"I bet Sarah would know," said Ava. She took her phone out of her pocket. "Do you think her mum has given her phone back yet? I'll try calling her."

Ava called Sarah's number. To her relief, Sarah answered. "Ava?"

Ava was so excited she didn't even pause to say hi. "Sarah, a nature spirit's woken up and is on the loose. Do you know what a conduit is?"

"A conduit is a channel that something can flow down but, hang on, what did you just say?" Sarah said. "There's a nature spirit on the loose?"

"Yes!" Ava told Sarah about how the face had

gone from the plaque. "Something must have woken it up and—"

"I bet it was the moonlight!" said Sarah quickly. "Do you remember, Lily read out something from the notebook about moonlight activating magic, particularly in stones and crystals. Well, the plaque was on the top shelf where the moonlight could shine on it."

"You're right," said Ava. "I moved it up there when I sorted the objects out after we sent the crocodile mummy back to sleep."

Sarah groaned. "That must be why your great-aunt wrote, *Be very careful where the curios are positioned.* Do you remember? We couldn't work out why it mattered – maybe the moonlight woke it up after the plaque was moved and it found a conduit of some kind."

"We've got to get it back into the plaque before anyone realizes what's going on," said Ava. "At the moment all the grown-ups seem to think the plants are growing because of the warm weather but that's not going to last for long."

"This is an emergency," said Sarah. "I don't like lying but we need to sort this out. I'll tell my mum we have a science project to do. I bet she'll let me come to yours if it's for school reasons. I'll ask then ring you back!"

She ended the call. Ava told Lily what Sarah had said and they waited anxiously, staring at Ava's phone.

"Please say yes, Auntie Ruth, please say yes," whispered Lily.

The phone rang. Ava answered it in a heartbeat. "Hello," she said.

"I can come round," Sarah said jubilantly. "Mum's not going to let me stay for long so make sure you've found out everything you possibly can about this spirit from the notebook. And, Ava…"

"Yeah?"

"Remember the time we caught the crocodile,

you had a really strong feeling that we needed to use the Aventurine Crystal? While you're waiting, why don't you see if any of the crystals tell you to use them this time?"

"That's a great idea," said Ava.

"I'll be at yours as soon as I can," promised Sarah.

✦

While Ava and Lily waited for Sarah, Lily scoured the notebook. "The notes are so random. On one page your great-aunt starts making notes about the crystals and then she'll put a note about one of the curios and then she'll break off from that to add a note about a different curio. Like this, look..." She pointed to a page where there was some hard to read writing and then a drawing and then some more notes. "She starts writing about how the Jasper Crystal can release and restore a spirit of fun and make people laugh and then she draws a picture of the plaque and then she puts a big star by it and an arrow which obviously means to go to a different page in the book." She flicked through the pages. "It's all such a jumble."

Leaving Lily to read through the notebook, Ava opened the box of crystals. Looking at them glittering in their compartments, Ava was sure Sarah was right and they should use a crystal to help them. But which one?

Shutting her eyes, she passed her hand slowly across the top, feeling the vibrations coming off them, some quick, some slow. Then she felt a sharp tingle. She paused and felt the palm of her hand getting warmer. Opening her eyes, she saw that her hand was over the Obsidian. *The Seeing Crystal,* she thought. Taking it out of the compartment, she slipped it into her pocket along with the necklace and pendant – they could be used to amplify a crystal's powers.

As she closed the lid of the box, she felt another sharp tingle and looked at the crystals. Her hand was near the spotty Jasper Stone. She smiled, remembering what had happened when they had taken it out before. She really didn't think they needed to fall about laughing and have their sense of fun restored and released while trying to capture an escaped nature spirit… She paused, a thought snagging in her brain. *Sense of fun…*

"Lily, what was that bit you read out of the notebook just now? The bit about the Jasper stone?" she said suddenly.

Lily flicked back. "Um … here it is. *The Jasper Crystal can release and restore a spirit of fun and make people—*"

"That's it," exclaimed Ava, interrupting her as she pictured what had happened the other day. "The Jasper was the conduit!"

"What do you mean?" said Lily, puzzled.

"You said earlier that the nature spirit is a fun-loving spirit. Well, think about what you just read. Jasper can *release a spirit of fun*!"

Lily still looked blank.

"When you were holding the Jasper crystal on Friday, you picked up the stone plaque and hid behind the desk with it," Ava went on. "I bet that when the Jasper touched the plaque, the spirit used it to escape out into the world."

"So, it's my fault?" said Lily, her hand flying to her mouth.

"No," Ava said quickly. "I was the one who moved the plaque into the moonlight and woke the spirit up in the first place."

Lily groaned. "There's so much we still need to learn about the curios, what to do, what not to do..."

"That'll have to wait," said Ava, seeing her reach for the notebook. "Right now, we need to catch the nature spirit before anyone finds out about it!"

There was a knock at the front door and they hurried to the hall. Sarah was on the doorstep with her mother. "Sarah!" Ava exclaimed. "Come in. We've got to get started on our project."

"I don't understand why you all left this project until the last minute," said Ruth. "What is it about?"

"Plants," said Ava quickly. "How they grow and where they grow. We'll need to do some research outside, maybe in the park," she added, thinking she'd better say that in case anyone spotted them outside. "Is that OK?" She crossed her fingers, praying that Ruth would say yes.

Ruth hesitated.

"Mum, there are no dangerous creatures here in England," Sarah said quickly. "Please let me go to the park."

Ruth gave in and nodded. "OK. Your project does sound interesting. Going to the park is fine, just no going into town on your own, all right?"

"Yes, I promise," said Sarah quickly.

"I'll come back and pick you up in two hours," said her mum.

"I could ring you when we're done?" said Sarah hopefully.

"No, two hours is enough," said Ruth. "You need to do some flute practice tonight."

"OK," sighed Sarah.

Ava shut the door. "Thank goodness you're here," she burst out.

"Tell me everything!" said Sarah excitedly.

They quickly explained what they had discovered.

"So, what do we do about this spirit now?" said Sarah.

"We find it, we catch it," said Ava. "Simple!"

CHAPTER NINE

Sarah stared at Ava. "But how do we catch it?"

Ava waved her hand impatiently. "We can figure that out as we go."

"But, Ava—"

"Sarah, we've only got two hours before you have to go home. We haven't got time to stand around talking. Come on," Ava urged.

Lily grabbed the notebook and Sarah put it and the box of crystals in her bag while Ava clipped on Pepper's lead before they set off. People were out in their front gardens cutting down creepers and pruning shrubs. Blossom covered the branches of the cherry trees that lined the road and butterflies fluttered through the air. The girls spotted Fin from their class in school taking photos of his sunflowers. They were even taller than Jack's now.

"Where should we start looking?" whispered Sarah.

"Let's follow the trail of things growing," said Ava.

They hurried down the road and crossed over to the riverside and the parkland beyond it. "The spirit could be anywhere," said Lily, gazing round. "Just look at this place."

The reeds had grown so much they were now clogging up the river, tulips were blooming in the flower beds alongside the roses, bracken was spreading out from under the trees and a carpet of grass had grown over the footpaths and cycle paths. As they watched, a cyclist almost fell off his bike as the wheels of his bike caught in a patch of brambles. An older woman was trying to untangle her little fluffy white dog from a pile of green sticky weed and a young man was hurrying past, his nose buried in a tissue as he sneezed loudly.

Ava looked around. The nature spirit had clearly been here but where was it now?

Suddenly Pepper gave a woof and leaped forwards, taking Ava by surprise. The lead slipped through her fingers. "Pepper! Come back!" she gasped as Pepper set off across the

park. Pepper ignored her, bounding through the long grass with her ears flapping. Ava, Sarah and Lily ran after her.

"Pepper!" they all shouted.

They stumbled and tripped as they ran through the long grass, sending clouds of butterflies flying up into the air. Ava realized Pepper was heading for a section of the park where some raised flower beds had been cleared of plants. The bare soil that filled them was a rich dark brown. "Pepper, what are you doing?"

Pepper stopped by the flower beds and started to bark frantically, jumping up and down on the spot.

Ava grabbed the lead and then gasped as she saw the bare soil starting to sprout with seedlings. First one flower bed and then the next and then the next. The little green shoots were pushing their way up through the soil, leaves unfurling before her eyes. It was like watching a speeded-up nature programme on TV or…

"Magic!" she gasped. "The spirit's here!"

"Where?" said Sarah, looking around.

"We can't see it. It must be invisible," said Ava. "But I bet Pepper can."

"How can we catch it, if we can't see it?" said Lily.

"This might help," said Ava, taking the

Obsidian Crystal out of her pocket and feeling energy tingling up her arm. The world went shadowy and dim but she could now see the vague green outline of a tall, thin figure spinning round on the bed they were watching, arms outstretched. "I can see it but not very clearly." Suddenly she knew what she had to do. "But if I put the Obsidian in the necklace I might be able to see it better."

She put the crystal into the middle of the triangular pendant, slotting it into the round centre. The black stone immediately started to sparkle. The spirit paused. Ava still couldn't see its face but she had a feeling it was now looking straight at them.

"Ava," said Sarah. "The seeds have stopped growing. What's the spirit doing?"

Ava gasped as the green figure suddenly shot towards them. It hissed at Pepper and then spun round the terrier in a circle. Pepper woofed in surprise as ivy suddenly started to grow up from the ground, tendrils twisting around her paws and tail. Before Ava could react, the spirit started spinning round her, Lily and Sarah. Creepers smothered their feet and twined up their legs.

Lily and Sarah yelled, pulling at the ivy and trying to get it off while Pepper growled and tried to bite at the leaves.

Ava put the necklace over her head and caught her breath as the fog finally cleared and she saw the nature spirit clearly. It had a pointed nose and mischievous black eyes, its skin was moss-green and its hair was made of vines. Its ragged clothes were as green as spring leaves and it was waving its hands at them, encouraging the creepers to grow higher. Its eyes met Ava's. She lunged forward to try to grab it but her hands passed clean through. The spirit grinned cheekily and then danced away, twirling and leaping on to the wall of the raised bed. With one sweep of its long fingers, the shoots burst upwards and turned into brightly coloured tulips.

With a final wink at Ava, it swirled away across the park, plants growing wherever it passed.

"It's gone," said Ava.

The creepers had stopped growing. The girls pulled them off their legs.

"What did it look like?" asked Sarah.

"Tall, thin, wild," said Ava, her thoughts racing. "And it went that way." She pointed into the distance. "Come on!"

"Ava, wait," said Sarah, grabbing her arm. "It's pointless. Even if we do catch up with it, how are we going to get it back to your house and into the plaque?"

"I don't know," Ava admitted.

"Let's go back to your house and try to come up with a plan," Sarah said to Ava.

"But..."

"I have to be at yours when my mum comes to get me. If I'm not she'll be upset and then she might not let me come round again," said Sarah.

"We can't risk it, Ava," Lily said.

Ava knew they were right. "OK, we'll go back and decide what to do," she sighed. She pulled off the necklace and glanced in the direction the spirit had gone. "But we'd better think fast!"

CHAPTER TEN

When they got back to Ava's house, they went to the Curio Room and sat on the sofa. Ava handed round a pack of cookies. "We need energy," she told them. "That nature spirit is seriously quick."

"Woof," said Pepper.

Ava grinned. "Yes, OK, you can have some energy too, Pepper." She gave the terrier a biscuit.

"I've found something!" Lily stabbed her finger at a page in the notebook. *"Nature spirits are attracted to all areas where things can grow but are particularly drawn to seeds and bulbs."*

"So, if we plant some seeds here then the nature spirit might come to us instead of us having to find it," said Ava thoughtfully.

"Good plan," said Sarah. "But how will we catch it when we see it?"

"A net?" Lily asked.

"No, it would just slip through the holes," said Ava. "How about a hoover. We could suck it up and trap it inside!"

"But a hoover won't work outside, it needs electricity," Sarah pointed out.

"One thing we must do before we try is

recharge the Obsidian Crystal," Lily pointed out. "We don't want it to run short of magic. We need to be able to see the spirit."

Ava nodded and, taking the Selenite wand out of the box, touched it to the Obsidian. It glowed brighter although not as bright as the Aventurine and Amethyst crystals had done when they'd been recharged in the light of the moon. Ava held the Selenite on it for sixty seconds. "All done," she said when the minute was up. She saw Sarah leafing through the notebook, frowning. "What is it?"

"The Selenite recharges positive energy but didn't a note in here say it also absorbs negative energy? Maybe it could absorb the nature spirit?"

Ava and Lily stared at her. "That might work," said Lily. "If we could touch the Selenite to the spirit then—"

"Kapow!" said Ava. "It might be absorbed into the Selenite. Then we just have to work out how to get it back into the plaque. Great idea! There are seeds and compost in the shed. Let's go!" She jumped to her feet. "Bring the book, Sarah."

Sarah shoved the notebook in her bag.

They were just about to go outside when there was a knock on the front door. Sarah's face fell. "That'll be my mum. You'll have to trap the spirit without me."

"Maybe we can persuade Auntie Ruth to let you stay," suggested Lily hopefully.

They went to the door. Ava's mum was just opening it. "Hello, Ruth, come in."

"Thank you," said Ruth. "But I can't stop. Sarah, it's time to go."

"Do I have to, Mum?" Sarah said. "Can't I stay a bit longer?"

"Please let her stay," begged Ava.

"Yes, please, Auntie Ruth," said Lily.

"It's fine by me," said Ava's mum.

Sarah's mum smiled. "That's very kind of you, Fran, but I think Sarah's spent enough time here this weekend. Come on, Sarah. Get your bag."

"No!" Sarah burst out stubbornly. "I don't want to, Mum!"

Her mum looked taken aback.

Sarah gave her mum a mutinous look. "I want to stay."

"Sarah!" Ruth said, looking hurt. "Why are you behaving like this?" Her eyes flicked to Ava as if she blamed her for Sarah arguing with her. "Please go and get your things like I've asked. I really don't want to have an argument about it."

Sarah let out an exclamation of frustration, grabbed her bag from the floor and stomped out.

"I'm sorry for Sarah's behaviour," Ruth apologized quickly to Ava's mum and then she hurried after her daughter.

"Oh dear." Ava's mum sighed as she shut

the door. "Poor Sarah. I don't think her mum's very happy with her."

"Sarah never normally argues with Auntie Ruth or Uncle Richard," said Lily.

Ava's mum kissed her hair. "At least you'll see her tomorrow at school."

Ava bit her lip. How could they trap the nature spirit while they were at school?

She and Lily walked slowly back into the Curio Room with Pepper. "What do we do now?" said Lily.

"We can't trap the spirit without Sarah, it wouldn't be fair. I'll text her and tell her we're going to wait until she's with us," said Ava, pulling out her phone.

Hope ur OK. We'll finish the project another time. Can u come round after skl tomorrow?

They waited a minute and then Sarah replied.

I bet Mum won't let me. She's rly mad. You'd better finish the project without me.

NO! Ava typed.

U have to!! U and Lily do the stuff we planned. Pls.

Are u sure?

Sarah sent Ava a row of thumbs up and then another text.

Btw I've still got the book in my bag. Soz. I'll bring it to skl tomorrow.

No probs, Ava replied.

K, I might read it and see if I can find anything else that might help us with the project. GOOD LUCK! Xxx

Ava showed the final message to Lily. "She wants us to try to trap the spirit without her."

"You know what? I think we should do as she says," said Lily. "We can't let it run around for another night. The adults are bound to start asking questions and we really don't want them finding out about the curios."

Ava picked up the Selenite. "You're right. This has to stop right now. Who knows how out of control the plants might get."

She and Lily headed outside. "Where should we plant the seeds?" Lily said.

Ava ran to the garden shed and staggered out with a huge flowerpot and a packet of seeds. "There's still some compost left over from yesterday," she said, plonking the pot down beside the shed door. "We can fill this pot, sow the seeds and then wait inside the shed. I'll wear the Obsidian crystal in the necklace and when I see the nature spirit appear, I'll jump out and touch it with the Selenite and then *zoom!* Hopefully the Selenite will absorb it."

"Brilliant!" said Lily excitedly.

They filled the pot with compost and planted the seeds, then Ava put the Obsidian into the necklace and they hid in the shed with Pepper. Ava held the Selenite wand out in front of her.

"It looks like a mini lightsaber," Lily said.

Ava grinned. "May the FOR-est be with me!"

They both giggled. "Shhh," said Lily. "The spirit could be here any minute."

The air in the shed smelled of fertilizer and compost. A collection of long-handled rakes and spades were leaning against one wall and on the shelves there were trowels, little plastic flowerpots, rolls of twine and packets of seeds, along with a big bag of salt that her mum used to make weedkiller.

"I bet the spirit wouldn't like that!" said Ava, pointing at it.

"Ava, concentrate," said Lily. "Tell me when you see the spirit."

Ava nodded, her eyes scanning the garden. Suddenly she felt Pepper stiffen and heard a low growl rumble through her.

"The spirit's here!" she hissed as the green figure came dancing across the garden. It spun and twirled as it headed straight towards the flowerpot. Pepper's growl grew louder. Ava cuddled her. "Shhh," she whispered, excitement sweeping through her. This was it! Was their plan going to work?

As the spirit reached the pot and bent down, its long fingers reaching out towards the soil, she heard the faint buzz of a phone.

"It's a voicemail from Sarah," Lily hissed. Should I listen to it? It might be important."

"No time," said Ava impatiently and she leaped out of the shed brandishing the Selenite wand. "Stop right there, Green Fingers," she shouted. Pepper barked loudly and darted at the spirit's heels.

The spirit raised its hands but Ava didn't give

it a chance to start growing plants around them. She jumped towards it, the Selenite outstretched.

"Ava, wait!" Lily gasped, appearing at the shed door with her phone in her hand.

But it was too late. The Selenite touched the spirit. It froze and then its face lit up with a huge grin as a glowing green light spread across its whole body. It started to spin faster and faster, growing taller and throwing its arms out, sending off glittering green sparks. Everywhere the sparks fell new plants grew but these weren't normal plants, these were giant, triffid-like plants with leaves as big as umbrellas. Ava staggered back. "Whoa!"

The spirit whirled away, spinning like a tornado, leaving a trail of the enormous plants behind it.

"What's happening?" Ava gasped.

Lily's face was pale. "I think we just made a big mistake."

"What do you mean?" Ava exclaimed.

Lily held up her phone. "Sarah's voicemail." She played it.

"*IMPORTANT! Do NOT touch the spirit with the Selenite wand! The book says the spirit's made of POSITIVE energy not negative. REMEMBER, the Selenite absorbs negative energy but it recharges positive energy, so touching it with the Selenite will recharge it and make it stronger…*"

Ava's eyes flew to Lily's. "Oh, pants!" she said in dismay. "What have I done?"

CHAPTER ELEVEN

"Quick," cried Ava, racing to the gate with Lily and Pepper hot on her heels.

The spirit danced away, flicking its long fingers and making vines shoot up from the soil, covering the houses and cars like green blankets and making trees burst through the tarmac with loud cracks. "There's no way anyone's going to believe global warming has caused this," said Lily.

"If we don't stop it, everyone's going to find out about the magic," said Ava as a sapling erupted in front of them through the pavement. She darted round it. "We've got to catch that spirit," she exclaimed, seeing it twirl across the road and into the park.

"I've got a text from Sarah," said Lily, pausing and quickly taking a photo of the street and sending it as a reply.

Ava started to run.

"Ava! Wait! Sarah's typing something!" Lily shouted.

Ava reluctantly stopped.

"*Use the spirit trap!*" Lily read out.

"What's she talking about?" said Ava in confusion.

"Hang on. She's typing more," said Lily.

But Ava was too impatient to wait. Pulling out her phone she phoned Sarah. The phone had barely rung once when Sarah picked it up. Ava switched it on to speaker as Sarah started to gabble.

"You need to use the spirit trap – the curio that looks like a little tennis racquet! I've been reading about it in the notebook. If you touch the spirit with it, the spirit will flow into it and if you say, '*I command you to remain*', it will stay in the spirit trap until you let it out with the words, '*Spirit, I release you*'. If you trap the nature spirit then we can try to work out how to release it and get it back into its plaque."

"Brilliant, Sarah," cried Ava.

"You're the best," cried Lily.

Ava ended the call and they raced back to her house. Ava grabbed the spirit trap from the shelf and handed it to Lily. "Here, can you put it in your bag?" As she did so, her phone buzzed with another text from Sarah.

I'm going to sneak out and help u with the project! I'll meet u at yours.

Ava hesitated. She desperately wanted Sarah to help. She was so good at thinking up plans and Ava really didn't want her to miss out on the adventure but what if Sarah's parents discovered she had gone? They'd be really worried. Ava quickly typed back.

NO!!! Ur parents will be upset. Lily and I can finish the project.

But I want to help!

I know but u have to stay home. Keep reading the notes and help us that way. PLS don't come. It's not worth it xxxxxx

There was a moment's pause and then a text appeared.

K. Followed by a sad face and a thumbs up. *Now stop wasting time. GO!!!*

Ava sent her a double thumbs up back. "Let's go and find that spirit," she said to Lily. "Before it turns the whole town into a giant jungle!"

✦

"There," Ava gasped as she and Lily stopped by the fountain in the square. They had run all the way, following the trail of triffid-like plants and trees. Pepper's tongue was hanging out as she panted on the end of her lead, too puffed out to even bark.

With the necklace on, Ava could see the nature spirit dancing along the top of the circular wall round the fountain pool. Huge water lilies were blooming on the water and pondweed was exploding over the wall. Behind them they could hear the squeal of brakes as cars tried to avoid the trees that had appeared in the road. Grass was pushing up through the cracks in the pavement and covering the cobbles. People were exclaiming in shock and filming on their phones as vines pushed up through the ground, twisting around the outdoor chairs and tables.

"What's going on?"

"I'm calling the police!" cried one of the café's waiters.

"Right, this ends now," muttered Ava. She marched towards the spirit, holding the spirit trap as if she was playing a tennis match. "Come here, you!"

The spirit stuck out its tongue and leaped off the fountain wall. It turned to whirl away down one of the alleys but Pepper had caught its scent. The terrier raced towards the alley entrance, blocking its path as she jumped up and down barking.

Ava expected the spirit to shoot past her but to her surprise a wary look crossed the spirit's face and it skidded to a stop and hissed at Pepper like a cat. "It doesn't like dogs!" Ava realized. "Good girl, Pepper," she shouted. "Stay!"

Miraculously, Pepper did as she was told for once.

The spirit turned to race off in the other

direction but Lily had seen Pepper barking and, guessing where the spirit was, she jumped into its path, brandishing two salt cellars she'd grabbed from a nearby table. "Oh no, you're not coming past me," she shouted, shaking the salt cellars. Salt flew into the air and Ava saw the spirit recoil in horror.

"Way to go, Lily!" she whooped.

Seeing the spirit momentarily distracted, Ava threw herself forward, sweeping the spirit trap in front of her. The head with its mesh of strings passed straight through the spirit but as it did so the spirit started to be sucked inside. It threw up its arms but it couldn't fight the spirit trap. Its whole body was sucked into it, swirling round and round like water going down a plughole. The spirit trap glowed green.

"I command you to remain!" gasped Ava and the glow faded. She swung round. "I caught it!" she gasped to Lily.

"You did?" said Lily.

"Yes! It's in here!" Ava brandished the spirit trap. Pepper raced over to her and jumped up, trying to sniff the trap. Ava handed it to Lily and then crouched down to hug the little terrier. "You were amazing, Pepper!" she said. Pepper put her paws on Ava's shoulders and licked her nose.

"Look, Ava," said Lily, gesturing round.

With the spirit trapped, the pondweed was retreating into the waters of the fountain, the lilies were closing up, the grass was being sucked back into the ground and the vines were shrinking. The people at the café tables were on their feet, pointing and shouting.

"Look what's happening!"

"The plants are disappearing!"

In the distance, Ava could hear the sounds

of cracks and thuds, which she hoped were the trees and triffids disappearing back into the ground beneath the tarmac of the road.

"Everything's going back to normal," said Lily in delight.

"We've got to call Sarah," said Ava. "She needs to know the spirit trap worked."

"On it," said Lily, already on her phone. "I'll video call her so she can see for herself."

Sarah's face appeared on Lily's screen. "What's going on? What's happened?"

"Look!" Lily held the phone up to show Sarah the square returning to normal. "The plants are disappearing!"

Ava waved the spirit trap at Lily's phone. "The spirit's in here!"

A beam spread across Sarah's face. "Awesome! Now all we need to do is work out how to get the spirit back into the plaque."

"We'll go to mine now," said Ava.

Sarah nodded. "Call me when you get there

so I can help you figure it—" She broke off as her bedroom door opened behind her. "Mum!" she said in alarm.

"Sarah, what are you doing?" they heard her mum say. "You're supposed to be practising your flute not talking to your friends. Honestly, I don't know what's got into you." She strode over and took the phone.

"But, Mum—" Ava and Lily heard Sarah say and then the screen went blank.

Ava looked at Lily, the fizzing happiness inside her fading away. "I hope we haven't got Sarah into even more trouble."

"Auntie Ruth did sound cross," said Lily anxiously.

Ava really wanted to do something to help but she had a feeling that turning up at Sarah's house would only make things worse.

"Let's go back to yours and work out what to do next," said Lily.

They walked home slowly. Although Ava was

delighted that the trees, vines and triffids had disappeared and the spring flowers had sunk back into the ground, she couldn't help worrying about Sarah. She hoped her mum wasn't too angry. They passed various groups of adults talking about what had happened. Ava caught snatches of the conversations.

"My money's on global warming."

"I heard it could have been the freak weather combined with the minerals in the soil round here."

"Strange things do seem to happen here in Eastwold, that's for sure!"

The other adults nodded.

A bit further on a group of teenage boys were clustered around a phone. "That is so fake!" one of them was hooting. "I mean, just look at those creepers growing in the square. They're totally plastic, anyone can see that!"

"Epic prank though," said the one holding the phone. "Apparently the police arrived in the square and there was nothing for them to see."

The boys walked off, still talking about it.

Ava glanced at Lily in relief. "Looks like we might have got away with keeping the magic secret."

"Only just though," said Lily. "If the spirit had been free for much longer, people would definitely have asked more questions."

"Well, let's just be glad the secret's still safe for now," said Ava. She lifted the spirit trap. "But we've got to work out how to get the spirit back into the plaque."

As they reached the gate of Curio House, there was the sound of a car pulling up behind them and a car door opening. "Ava! Lily!"

Hearing Sarah's voice, they swung round in surprise. Sarah jumped out and ran to them, happiness radiating from her.

Ava couldn't believe it. What was going on?

Ruth got out of the driver's side and came over. "Ava..." She cleared her throat.

Ava tensed. Was she about to be told off?

But to her surprise, Sarah's mum smiled. "I want to thank you for being a good friend to Sarah."

"Um… OK," Ava said astonished.

"After I found Sarah talking to you and Lily earlier, I took her phone and I read the messages between the two of you. Thank you for telling Sarah she shouldn't leave the house without permission. That was very sensible and I'm very glad Sarah decided to listen to you. This project you're all working on is obviously very important to you and because Sarah made the right choice earlier I'm letting her come round for a few hours so you can finish it off."

"Oh!" said Ava.

"Thank you, Auntie Ruth!" said Lily, running over and hugging her.

"Yes, thanks, Mum!" said Sarah, joining in. Pepper bounded over too, standing on her back legs.

Ruth gave a slightly nervous laugh and patted Pepper gingerly on the head. "Good dog. Right, I'll see you in a few hours, Sarah."

Sarah and Lily joined Ava and they all ran into the garden with Pepper trotting beside them. "Can you believe it?" said Sarah. "I thought Mum was going to be really annoyed when she saw the messages but she came in and told me she was glad I'd been sensible. And now I'm here!"

Lily grinned. "And your mum seems to think Ava is great."

"The important thing is you're here and we can work out how to get the spirit back into the plaque together," said Ava jubilantly. "Come on!"

✦

"So, what do we do?" said Lily a few minutes later when they stood in the Curio Room with the stone plaque and the spirit trap on the desk. "How do we get the spirit from the trap to the plaque without it escaping?"

They all stared at the curios as if hoping inspiration would come to them.

"Sarah, have you got a plan?" said Ava hopefully.

"Sorry, no," Sarah sighed.

"Lily?"

"No idea," said Lily.

"Pepper?" said Ava.

Pepper had her front paws on the desk and was sniffing at the box of crystals.

"I'm talking to you, Pepper," Ava said, mock strictly. "Don't ignore me. What do you think we should—" She broke off as she saw what Pepper was sniffing at. "The crystals!" she said. "Maybe they can help!"

"How?" said Lily.

Ava opened the box, her gaze falling on the purple Amethyst Crystal that she'd been longing to try out again. "The Amethyst. It brings what you desire. Well, I desire a way of getting the spirit back into the plaque!"

"Try it," said Sarah eagerly.

Taking the Amethyst out of the box, Ava felt warmth flood along her fingers and up her arm. She shut her eyes, letting everything else fade as she focused on the crystal in her hand, the way it was vibrating, the warmth she was feeling. The power felt amazing.

I want a way to send the spirit back into the plaque, she thought. *We have to stop it before it does any more damage.*

A rattling noise made her open her eyes. It was coming from the shelves. Turning she saw the bottle of ancient seeds shaking slightly on the shelf, the seeds rattling against the glass. She frowned. What was happening?

"The seeds!" gasped Lily. "Do you remember the notebook said nature spirits love anything that can grow. I bet it'll love these old seeds!"

"If we put the seeds into the hole in the plaque, maybe it'll follow them in there," said Ava.

"But how do we keep it inside?" said Sarah.

"We could say the words I used to stop it leaving the spirit trap," said Ava. "And then we can touch the Osiris Stone to send it back to sleep. It worked on the crocodile mummy, maybe it will work on a nature spirit too!" She looked at the others, her heart beating faster with excitement. "It's worth a try, isn't it?"

They nodded eagerly. Ava fetched the glass bottle, removed the cork and emptied the seeds out on to the desk. They were small, hard and brown. Lily read the faded label that was hanging around the neck of the bottle. "*Seeds of the extinct afypnistis flower from Ancient Greece. The seeds and flowers possess the ability to attract and awaken spirits.*"

"If the seeds attract spirits that's perfect," said Ava excitedly. She picked up the seeds and posted them into the hole in the plaque where the spirit's mouth had been.

Then she picked up the spirit trap. "OK,

here goes! What was it I had to say?"

"*Spirit, I release you,*" Sarah told her.

Ava took a breath and in the most commanding voice she could manage, exclaimed, "Spirit, I release you!" She gave the spirit trap a dramatic flourish. It started to glow green and suddenly the spirit came spiralling out like a genie from a bottle. It grew and grew. Pepper started to bark furiously. But then the spirit's eyes turned to the stone plaque. A look of greedy delight filled its face and it shot towards the stone and disappeared inside.

As the last of it disappeared into the stone, Ava grabbed the plaque. "Spirit, I command you to remain!"

The plaque started to shake in her hands. Shoots covered with buds burst out through the hole in the centre, opening into white star-shaped flowers with a gold dot on every petal. "Whoa," Ava gasped, holding on as the plaque shook harder and harder and the shoots twined around her hands. "The Osiris Stone!" she cried. "Quick!"

Sarah touched the plaque with the dark side of the stone. The plaque slowly stopped shaking, the flower heads shut and retreated inside, leaving just a single white petal clinging to the stone surface.

"The face, Ava!" said Lily, pointing.

Ava gasped as she realized that the nature spirit's face had reappeared in the plaque again but now with its eyes closed. They'd trapped the spirit *and* they had managed to send it back to sleep.

"We did it!" she cried, putting the plaque on one of the lower shelves, pushing it to the back where it would be safely shielded from the light of the moon. She took the necklace off and put both the Obsidian and Amethyst crystals back into the box.

Sarah dropped the Osiris Stone carefully into its compartment too and shut the lid. "I can't believe it's over. That was awesome!" she said.

"TREE-mendous!" said Lily, her eyes sparkling.

"We TREE-umphed over the nature spirit!" said Ava with a grin.

"We should get TREE-shirts!" Sarah joined in.

They all burst out laughing. The door opened and Ava's mum looked in. "It sounds like you're having quite a party in here. Can I join in?"

"Sure," said Ava, going over and giving her mum a hug. "Cos you know what? You're simp-TREE the best mum ever!"

Her mum looked a bit confused but hugged her back, smiling. "Love you too, sweetie, and talking of trees, did you hear what happened with the plants in town today? They all suddenly started to grow."

"I know. I wonder why that happened?" said Ava innocently.

"No one knows for sure," her mum agreed. "But apparently it only lasted a few minutes and everything seems to be back to normal now so people think it must have just been some kind of freak occurrence. It's very strange though and quite worrying. I'm glad you were all OK."

"Yeah, imagine if a ginormous tree had grown up underneath us and swept us into the air," said Ava.

Her mum laughed. "I don't think it would have quite come to that but it is strange. I mean, why did the plants just grow like that then disappear?"

Ava decided it might be best to change the subject. "Can I smell cake, Mum?"

Her mum's thoughtful frown became a smile. "You can," she said. "I've just made some cupcakes. If you want some, come through to the kitchen. I just need to add a few chocolate sprinkles."

"Thanks, Mum!" called Ava as her mum left. She turned to the others. "Perfect! We've saved the day and we get to have cake too!"

"This has been such an awesome adventure," said Sarah happily. "The nature spirit has gone back to sleep and hopefully, from now on, my mum will be a little more relaxed about me doing stuff with you."

"I bet it'll help now that she likes Ava," said Lily.

"Told you I'd win her round," said Ava with a grin. "Race you both to the kitchen! Last one there is a smelly spirit!"

As they raced out of the room and the door slammed shut behind them, the single white petal that had been clinging to the stone plaque broke free. It floated up into the air and then drifted down, coming to land on one of the curios below...

Keep reading for
a sneak peek at the
Magic Keepers' next
adventure...

CHAPTER ONE

Ten magic crystals glimmered as they nestled in their individual compartments in the old leather box on the desk. Watched eagerly by her best friends Lily and Sarah and her dog Pepper, Ava moved her hand over the top, her palm not quite touching the crystals. She could feel them all faintly vibrating. Some released sharp pulses of energy, others were long and soothing or tingly and tickly. Excitement swept through her. Which one should she choose to do magic with? The soft pink Rose Quartz? The glittering purple Amethyst? The glowing green Jade?

Ava's stomach fizzed at the thought of doing magic. She could still hardly believe how much her life had changed in the last six weeks. She and her mum had moved house, she'd started a new school and she'd met Lily and Sarah. But best of all she'd made the amazing discovery that magic was real!

It had all begun when Ava's mum had inherited Curio House and its contents from her great-aunt Enid who had been a famous archaeologist. Curio House was a huge, crumbling Victorian villa with eight bedrooms and a large walled garden, and in one of the rooms there was a collection of unusual old objects called curios. Ava, Lily and Sarah had found out that all the curios were magic in some way and that Great-Aunt Enid had been keeping their magic secret. The girls were determined to keep it secret too. The last thing they wanted was someone taking the collection away!

However, it wasn't always easy. First, a baby

crocodile mummy had come to life and they'd had to catch it after it escaped from the house. Then an ancient nature spirit had left its stone plaque to cause chaos in town, making plants and trees grow everywhere, until they managed to trap it and send it back to sleep. Being magic keepers was a lot of work but it was also a lot of fun!

Along with the curios, Great-Aunt Enid had left a box of *'Magyck Crystals for the Protection of the Magyck Curios'*. The girls had used the crystals to help in their last two adventures but they were still finding out how the crystals worked. They had decided to go to Ava's house after school that day to practise controlling the magic.

Ava's fingers paused as they passed over a dark grey stone with patches of deep red. She felt like the stone was reaching out to her, urging her to use it. "I'm going to try this one," she announced, picking it up.

"That's the Bloodstone, we used it when we first discovered the crystals were magic," said Lily, pushing her hair behind her ears. She and Sarah were cousins but they looked very different – Lily had shiny black hair and dark brown eyes whereas Sarah had chin-length blonde hair and blue eyes. They had very different personalities too.

Lily now picked up the box. Great-Aunt Enid had written notes about the crystals on the inside of the lid in her tiny, cramped handwriting. *"Bloodstone,"* she read out. *"The Enhancing Crystal. Bloodstone increases energy and courage. It also enhances physical powers and decision-making."*

Sarah had a notebook ready and a pen in her hand. "Why did you choose that particular crystal, Ava?" She was very scientific and loved finding things out.

Ava shrugged. It was like trying to explain why you liked one colour more than another. "It just felt right."

"But why exactly?" pressed Sarah. "Can you be more specific?"

"Nope," said Ava. She couldn't explain it but some things just felt right or wrong. Sometimes she sensed something bad was about to happen, or she could instinctively tell if a person or animal was ill or in trouble. Her mum said it was because she was very intuitive. It seemed to make it easy for her to do magic – the crystals always worked more quickly for her than for the others.

Sarah made a note. "OK, well, now you've picked it, why don't you see how well you can control the magic?"

Ava focused on the crystal, letting everything else fade away – the high-ceilinged room with its dusty bookcases and shelves full of curios, the huge sash windows framed by velvet curtains, the faded rugs on the wooden floor and the old sofas. Even her friends and her Tibetan terrier Pepper – who was lying on a chair, watching her through her shaggy fringe – disappeared. Ava felt the crystal's energy merging with hers and she caught her breath.

Also by Linda Chapman

Also by Linda Chapman

ABOUT THE AUTHOR

Linda Chapman is the best-selling author of over 200 books. The biggest compliment Linda can receive is for a child to tell her they became a reader after reading one of her books.

Linda lives in a cottage with a tower in Leicestershire with her husband, three children, three dogs and two ponies. When she's not writing, Linda likes to ride, read and visit schools and libraries to talk to people about writing.

www.lindachapmanauthor.co.uk

ABOUT THE ILLUSTRATOR

Giang has been working as a children's book illustrator for more than ten years. She works in a studio with her partner and three cats. She also loves comics and graphic novels, and dreams of one day finding the time to make her own comic series. Nowadays she tries to practise yoga so that she can keep her back fine after a long time of it being not so fine.